Flames

A Musical Thriller

Book, Music, and Lyrics by
Stephen Dolginoff

A SAMUEL FRENCH ACTING EDITION

FOUNDED 1830

SAMUELFRENCH.COM
SAMUELFRENCH-LONDON.CO.UK

FOR PRODUCTION ENQUIRIES

UNITED STATES AND CANADA
Info@SamuelFrench.com
1-866-598-8449

UNITED KINGDOM AND EUROPE
Plays@SamuelFrench-London.co.uk
020-7255-4302

Each title is subject to availability from Samuel French, depending upon country of performance. Please be aware that FLAMES may not be licensed by Samuel French in your territory. Professional and amateur producers should contact the nearest Samuel French office or licensing partner to verify availability.

MUSIC USE NOTE

Licensees are solely responsible for obtaining formal written permission from copyright owners to use copyrighted music in the performance of this play and are strongly cautioned to do so. If no such permission is obtained by the licensee, then the licensee must use only original music that the licensee owns and controls. Licensees are solely responsible and liable for all music clearances and shall indemnify the copyright owners of the play(s) and their licensing agent, Samuel French, against any costs, expenses, losses and liabilities arising from the use of music by licensees. Please contact the appropriate music licensing authority in your territory for the rights to any incidental music.

RENTAL MATERIALS

An orchestration consisting of a **Piano/Vocal score**, **Vocal books**, and an **Instrumental CD** will be loaned two months prior to the production ONLY on the receipt of the Licensing Fee quoted for all performances, the rental fee and a refundable deposit. Please contact Samuel French for perusal of the music materials as well as a performance license application.

IMPORTANT BILLING AND CREDIT REQUIREMENTS

If you have obtained performance rights to this title, please refer to your licensing agreement for important billing and credit requirements.

FLAMES was originally produced at LAMB Arts Regional Theatre in Sioux City, Iowa (Russell Wooley, Managing/Artistic Director/Producer; Diana Wooley, Producer), opening on October 17, 2013. The director was Russell Wooley; the musical direction was by Donald E. Short III; the fight direction was by Eric Hagen; the set & sound design was by Russell Wooley; the lighting design was by Michael Rohlena; the costume design was by Karen Sowienski; the stage manager was Bronwyn Eastlick. The piano arrangements were by Stephen Dolginoff and Zachary Orts. The cast was as follows:

MEREDITH . . . . Jessica Wheeler

ERIC . . . . Matt Rixner

EDMOND . . . . Josh Case

CHARACTERS

MEREDITH – a beautiful woman in her late 20s-early 30s.
ERIC – a handsome man in his 30s.
EDMOND – a non-descript man in his 30s.

SETTING

A cemetery (and various flashback locales)

TIME

The present (and flashbacks to the recent past)

AUTHOR'S ACKNOWLEDGEMENTS

Special thanks to Zachary Orts,
Jim Kierstead, Camille Diamond, Joshua Rivedal, Vincent Teschel,
Jason Rockwood, Seth Arrobas, Melinda Berk, Nicole Del Percio,
Moritz Staemmler, Bernd Julius Arends,
Russell & Diana Wooley, Donny Short,
Amy Rose Marsh, Amy Wagner, and Ron Gwiazda

MUSICAL NUMBERS

PRELUDE

"HE CAN STILL HEAR YOU" – Eric

"YOU'RE DIFFERENT" – Meredith

"IDENTIFIED THE BODY" – Meredith and Edmond

"JEALOUSY" – Eric

"NIGHT OF THE FIRE (ERIC'S VERSION)" – Eric and Edmond

"NIGHT OF THE FIRE (EDMOND'S VERSION)" – Edmond and Eric

"THE RIGHT CHOICE" – Meredith

"NEVER LET HIM HURT YOU" – Edmond

REPRISE: "NIGHT OF THE FIRE" – Eric

"EDMOND'S EYES" – Eric

FINALE – Eric and Meredith*

(*A printed program shouldn't reveal who sings the finale.)

AUTHOR'S NOTES

FLAMES is a musical suspense thriller that takes place in a dark, moody setting, and should be performed in a cautious and careful pace to keep the tension high. The show features three very modern characters in a very gothic setting. The more their costumes are in stark contrast to the cemetery atmosphere, the better. And though the story is in no way supernatural, it should be presented to almost have the tone of a ghost story combined with a mystery. Like "Alfred Hitchcock meets Edgar Allan Poe."

Several moments are marked in the script as "flashbacks" because they take place in the past as told by one of the characters. "Flashback" is not an accurate word for most of these scenes. In most cases, a character is telling a story of what they *claim* happened in the past. Whether or not it is true isn't revealed until the end. But the audience in the theatre should perceive these scenes as "flashbacks" as they unfold.

In the script there is a character named "Edmond" – by the end it will be revealed whether or not this man is only *pretending* to be "Edmond" or really is him. But for purposes of clarity, his character shall always have that name in the script. The character of Meredith is often referred to by the nickname "Mere" – it is pronounced like "Mare."

Great care should be taken when casting the role of Edmond in order to keep the mystery continuity strong. It is best if he is handsome, yet in an average, non-descript kind of way. It is only his eyes that Meredith recognizes at first and Eric comments on later. If the actor has very distinguishing physical characteristics such as red hair and freckles, or if he is extraordinarily tall, short, etc., then Meredith will have much more information to use to prove or disprove his story. The possibility that he is telling the truth is very important. So nothing in his appearance should run counter to that. Remember, it is very dark and rainy. The trees cast shadows. Meredith appears to be in a fragile state-of-mind. So the illusion that this man may be telling the truth is a little easier to believe than if it were broad daylight.

It is crucial to always keep the audience guessing. All three characters are pretending to be something they're not to some extent. And they all end up vastly different than how they start. Like in a typical suspense thriller, the audience should never quite get a handle on exactly what is going on until the end. One minute Eric seems like the romantic hero, and then in Edmond's flashbacks, Eric is more of an unstable psychopath. And vice versa! Meredith appears to be a standard ingénue/woman-in-jeopardy, so her ultimate reveal should be quite a surprise.

In the original production, the fights, strangulations, bodies rising back up, bloody umbrella stab, etc. were staged with great precision. And they were choreographed extremely carefully to appear very realistic, and quite frightening. With all the lightning and thunder going on around them, it was extremely effective.

Most importantly, have fun! These three characters end up doing horrible things to each other live onstage, so please revel in the outrageousness.

– Stephen Dolginoff

[MUSIC NO. 1 – "PRELUDE"]

(While the houselights are still up, an enormous clap of thunder plunges the audience into total darkness.

Prelude music immediately begins and sets an eerie, atmospheric mood.

Within the music, there is another clap of thunder and a flash of lightning. This illumination causes us to briefly glimpse an empty cemetery.

The music continues in the darkness.

Another clap of thunder and lightning, this time fleetingly revealing the figures of a **MAN** *and a* **WOMAN**, *under an umbrella, entering the cemetery, while being slowed by the storm.*

The music continues in the darkness and then ends as the storm softly abates.)

The Cemetery, Night – The Present.

(Lights finally fade up on a small, dark, traditionally spooky cemetery.

It is a murky, stormy night under an ominous full moon.

There are gravestones of varying sizes, a few small monuments, trees, tree stumps, perhaps a marble bench or two.

[Alternatively, it could be set with nothing but a single gravestone on a bare stage or black box.]

MEREDITH, *a woman in her late 20's-early 30s; and* **ERIC**, *a man in his 30s, both wearing stylish raincoats,* *stand huddled under a large, old-fashioned, black, metal-tipped, umbrella. In front of them is a gravestone, which simply reads: "Edmond."*

There is another flash of lightning and a clap of thunder, but it sounds more distant. They both look up at the sky.

After a few moments, **ERIC** *speaks.)*

ERIC. It looks like that's the last of the storm.

MEREDITH. Thank God. Finally. I'm so terrified of lightning. Ever since I was little. I was always afraid I was gonna get shocked.

ERIC. There's nothing to be scared of, Mere. *(pronounced "Mare")*

(They put down the umbrella.)

At least it was a good excuse to carry Edmond's old umbrella.

MEREDITH. *(as she's closing it)* I never need an excuse. It reminds me of him. Classic.

(He smiles at her warmly.)

ERIC. Here, take one.

*(***ERIC** *takes out two small memorial candles and hands one to her. They kneel down at Edmond's grave and place them in front of it.*

Then **ERIC** *takes out a book of matches and they each light their candle. The flames cast long shadows onto the gravestone.)*

MEREDITH. It's hard to believe he's been gone for a whole year.

*(***MEREDITH** *starts to cry.* **ERIC** *tries to console her.)*

ERIC. I know.

MEREDITH. We'll be together again someday, Edmond.

ERIC. I hope you're resting in peace, buddy.

*(***MEREDITH** *composes herself.)*

MEREDITH. Thanks for bringing me here tonight, Eric.

ERIC. Sometimes I have good ideas.

MEREDITH. This is just like the funeral. Only you and me. No one else came.

ERIC. That's the past. It doesn't matter anymore. We were there for him then. And we're here for him now.

MEREDITH. It wasn't much of a surprise that no one wanted to be here after what he did. How he died…what a horrible way to go.

(She gets up, **ERIC** *follows and tries to comfort her.)*

ERIC. Meredith…don't talk about that now. It's over. We have to just…remember the good.

MEREDITH. One day he was a successful guy without a care in the world. The next day a criminal, and then… dead.

ERIC. I know. It was so fast.

MEREDITH. I still don't understand, Eric. Why did he do it? Those people – he may as well have murdered them.

ERIC. Don't say that. You know it was a far cry from murder. There's no other explanation – he just needed the money. And then he got carried away.

MEREDITH. He spent too much on me. Why didn't he just tell me he was having problems? Why didn't he confide in you?

ERIC. He probably thought I wouldn't understand.

MEREDITH. *I* would have understood. I loved him.

ERIC. I loved him too. He was like a brother.

MEREDITH. All that money…just gone without a trace.

ERIC. It isn't right.

MEREDITH. I keep looking at that horrible wedding dress in my closet. Haunting me. Tormenting me. He'll never see how I looked in it.

ERIC. You will get over this. I promise.

MEREDITH. *(being irrational)* How? Why?

ERIC. Because that's what Edmond wants.

(Music begins.)

MEREDITH. He's gone. He can't want anything anymore.

ERIC. Not as long as we remember him. In a way, he's still with us…

MEREDITH. *(near tears)* Did we even know him?

ERIC. Shhh….

(He sings.)

[MUSIC NO. 2 – "HE CAN STILL HEAR YOU"]

YOU CAN'T LET BAD KARMA
ENTER YOUR MIND
AND TRY TO STEER YOU.
AS LONG AS HE'S IN YOUR HEART,
YOU WILL FIND
HE CAN STILL HEAR YOU.

HIS PRESENCE IS STRONG
SO YOU CAN LET GO.
YOU MAY FIND THE CONCEPT STRANGE,
BUT I KNOW
HE CAN STILL HEAR YOU.

HIS PICTURES ARE LOOKING DOWN
FROM YOUR WALL,
HE'LL ALWAYS BE NEAR YOU.
BUT WHY SHOULD YOUR WORLD
SLOW DOWN TO A CRAWL?
HE CAN STILL HEAR YOU.

YOU DON'T EVER
HAVE TO BLOW OUT THE FLAME
BUT DON'T SHUT ME OUT,
I'M FEELING THE SAME.
HE CAN STILL HEAR YOU.

(He moves in closer to her.)

SO LET'S GET SOME PERSPECTIVE,
YOU HAVE TO LIVE YOUR LIFE.

IT'S HARD TO BE OBJECTIVE
BUT I'M STANDING HERE AND WAITING,
IF YOU'LL LET ME TAKE YOUR HAND
AND CONSIDER MAYBE DATING–
HE'D UNDERSTAND.

(Music continues.)

MEREDITH. I can't say you're surprising me. And it's crossed my mind too. But, it just doesn't feel right.

ERIC. Why not? We're all we have left, Mere. He'd want us to be happy.

MEREDITH. He'd want us to forgive him. And mourn him.

ERIC. And we have. For a *year*.

(He continues to sing.)

YOU KNOW THAT HE'S STILL
ALIVE IN MY HEAD,
AS LONG AS YOU'RE NEAR ME.
YOU KNOW THAT I HOLD
RESPECT FOR THE DEAD.
HE CAN STILL HEAR ME.

I KNOW THAT HE WANTS
MY HAPPINESS TOO,
I KNOW HE SUPPORTS
WHAT I'D LIKE TO DO,
SO LET ME EXPLORE
MY FEELINGS FOR YOU …

I CAN GIVE YOU THE MOON
AND IT ISN'T TOO SOON
IF YOU THINK IT THROUGH!

(Music continues.)

MEREDITH. Eric…

ERIC. We've grown so close this year.

MEREDITH. I know. And I've depended on you. More than I should have.

ERIC. No. Exactly like you should have.

(He takes a tentative step toward her. Then takes her in his arms gently to give her a kiss.

Before their lips meet **MEREDITH** *pulls back.)*

MEREDITH. You're vibrating.

ERIC. What? Oh damn.

(He fishes into his coat pocket, pulls out a large tablet-style smartphone, and checks the screen.)

ERIC. *(cont.)* There's no way to escape e-mail. Sorry.

(He turns off the smartphone and puts it back into his pocket.

Then he reaches for her again and kisses her softly and briefly.)

ERIC. That's what I've been waiting for.

MEREDITH. I wasn't expecting that tonight.

(She motions to **EDMOND** *'s grave.)*

In front of Edmond.

ERIC. But, doesn't it feel good?

MEREDITH. I'm not sure yet.

ERIC. I can give you time.

MEREDITH. That's what I need.

(She goes to the gravestone.)

MEREDITH. Do you think you could let me be alone here for awhile?

ERIC. Actually, that's a great idea. Stay here and talk to Edmond about it. And see how *he* feels.

MEREDITH. *(confused)* What?

(She catches on.)

Oh…because he can still…

*(***ERIC** *smiles.)*

ERIC. *(sings)*
YOU KNOW THAT HIS AURA
STILL FILLS THE AIR.

SO TALK TO HIM NOW;
HE'LL LISTEN, I SWEAR.
HE CAN STILL HEAR YOU,
HE CAN STILL HEAR YOU,
HE'S RIGHT THERE.

(Music ends.)

MEREDITH. *(looking at the grave)* He is.

ERIC. And there's no better place for you to be.

(He squeezes her hand and notices her ring.)

You still wear your engagement ring. I was with him the day he bought it. The day before he...

(He starts to get choked up.)

Don't you think it's time to take it off?

MEREDITH. Only a man would say that. I haven't taken this ring off since he put it on my finger. He made me promise him I never would.

ERIC. I remember him telling me he was gonna say that. So romantic.

MEREDITH. I didn't realize that was the very last time I would ever see him alive.

ERIC. *(agreeing, sadly)* He was ... gone by the end of that night.

MEREDITH. So I'll never take it off, no matter where I am, no matter what I'm doing. It's all I have left.

ERIC. Well, maybe someday you'll have a new ring. From someone important.

(He holds her hand and touches the ring. She pulls it away.)

MEREDITH. Then it will sit right next to this one.

ERIC. Of course.

(Realizing he has offended her, he moves to exit.)

I'll ... get some herbal tea at that diner down the road.

MEREDITH. That creepy place?

(ERIC looks around at their surroundings as thunder is heard.)

ERIC. It's no creepier than here.

MEREDITH. I still don't think I'd drink their tea.

(He chuckles and hugs her.)

ERIC. Meet me there when you're finished.

MEREDITH. Alright. I won't be long.

ERIC. *(heading off)* I'll see you in a bit.

(He exits.

She takes off her coat, then clutches at her ring and twists it around her finger as she speaks to the grave.)

MEREDITH. Edmond. Eric's right. I have to go on with my life. I miss you so much. But every day it does get a little easier. And right now I need to be very sure that I'm doing what you'd want.

[MUSIC NO.3 – EDMOND'S ENTRANCE UNDERSCORE]

*(A **MAN** in his 30s, dressed in dark clothing, slowly enters from the shadows behind her, accompanied by a few strains of mysterious music.*

He watches her for a moment and walks toward the grave.

Thunder clap. A flash of lightning finally illuminates him fully.

MEREDITH *jumps.)*

MAN (EDMOND). Hello.

MEREDITH. Damn. You frightened me.

MAN (EDMOND). I'm so sorry.

MEREDITH. Not your fault. It's a public place.

(She tries to be polite.)

Hello.

MAN (EDMOND). I didn't mean to interrupt you.

MEREDITH. It's fine. It was a one sided conversation anyway.

*(As **MEREDITH** watches him, he goes to the gravestone and blows out both candles.)*

MEREDITH. Why did you do that?

MAN (EDMOND). Open flames are dangerous.

MEREDITH. They're just candles. And they were *mine.*

MAN (EDMOND). I'm sorry.

(She moves to re-light them, but realizes she doesn't have the matches.)

MEREDITH. Have you got a match?

MAN (EDMOND). No.

MEREDITH. *(referring to the grave)* Maybe it's better. It's how he died. Fire.

MAN (EDMOND). I know.

MEREDITH. You do? You came to visit Edmond?

MAN (EDMOND). Yes.

MEREDITH. You knew him?

MAN (EDMOND). Yes.

MEREDITH. I was his fiancée. I have no idea who you are. Did you work together?

MAN (EDMOND). I wanted to see his grave.

MEREDITH. I'm sorry, but who are you?

MAN (EDMOND). Is your boyfriend coming back?

MEREDITH. Eric? He's not my …who are you?

MAN (EDMOND). That's not an easy question to answer.

MEREDITH. You're freaking me out.

MAN (EDMOND). Don't be afraid.

MEREDITH. Just tell me who the hell you are. If you knew Edmond, you'd know that he didn't end up with any friends. So it's difficult for me to believe that you…

MAN (EDMOND). Mere, it's me.

*(**MEREDITH** just stares at him.)*

MEREDITH. You know my name?

MAN (EDMOND). It's *me.*

MEREDITH. It's who?

MAN (EDMOND). Look at my eyes. You always said you loved my eyes.

MEREDITH. What the hell are you talking about?

(The **MAN** *looks to the gravestone pointedly.)*

MAN (EDMOND). It's *me*. Look.

MEREDITH. I don't know who you are, but I think you should leave now.

(He carefully moves closer to her.)

EDMOND. You know who I am. Just look.

*(***MEREDITH** *looks into his eyes.)*

MAN (EDMOND). Remember the first night you looked into them?

(He removes his overcoat.

The lights begin to change.)

[MUSIC NO.4 – FIRST FLASHBACK INTRO]

Flashback. A Bar. Two Years Earlier.

(Music begins and underscores the scene, as **MEREDITH** *and* **EDMOND** *share a flashback to the night the couple first met.*

[And though she isn't sure this **MAN** *really is him, he acts as* **EDMOND** *in the flashback.]*

The scenery doesn't change. We are still in the cemetery, only disguised by lighting.

If desired, furniture can rise up in a swirl of mist, as if from a grave, and do the same for all flashback scenes. But it is not necessary to have any additional set pieces.

MEREDITH *and* **EDMOND** *are in a dark bar/dance club, with club-style lighting moving all around them. He approaches her.)*

MAN (EDMOND). Meredith, right?

MEREDITH. That's right.

MAN (EDMOND). *(very charming)* We met last week. But, you were on your way out.

MEREDITH. I remember.

(She is clearly smitten by him.)

MAN (EDMOND). I was hoping we'd run into each other again.

MEREDITH. Me too.

MAN (EDMOND). I'd like to learn more about you.

MEREDITH. *(coyly)* What do you want to know?

(He contemplates for a moment and smiles.)

MAN (EDMOND). Everything.

(MEREDITH *takes in his dreamy, romantic quality. Music intensifies, she sings.)*

[MUSIC NO.5 – "YOU'RE DIFFERENT"]

MEREDITH.

I'M A GIRL WHO DOESN'T LIKE
BLUE JEANS OR LEATHER
OR AN EVENING WATCHING FOOTBALL
WITH A BEER.
ALL THE GUYS I MEET
CAN'T STRING FOUR WORDS TOGETHER.
SO ON WEEKENDS, WITH MY FRIENDS
I WIND UP HERE!

I'M A GIRL WHO LIKES TO CUDDLE
WITH MY KITTEN
BUT WITH MEN,
I FIND THAT NEVER REALLY FLIES.
AND ALTHOUGH MY
DATING POLICY'S UNWRITTEN,
I DO NOTHING ELSE

BUT ALWAYS COMPROMISE.

BUT YOU'VE STILL GOT ALL YOUR HAIR
AND YOU SEEM TO REALLY CARE
YOU'RE DIFFERENT FROM THE OTHER GUYS
AND FOR ME THAT'S RARE!

(He smiles at her, somewhat embarrassed by her compliments.)

I'M A GIRL WHO BUYS A BOOK
THEN BUYS ANOTHER.
AND I LISTEN TO THE CLASSICS,
LOVE GOOD FLICKS.
TRY TO FIND A GUY WHO
DOESN'T WANT A MOTHER
OR A GUY WHO ISN'T ONLY OUT FOR KICKS.

BUT YOUR MANNERS ALL ARE THERE
AND YOU'VE SURE GOT LOOKS TO SPARE.
YOU'RE DIFFERENT FROM THE OTHER GUYS
AND FOR ME THAT'S RARE!

(He takes her into his arms and they start dancing. She looks deeply into his eyes.)

HOW DID YOUR ARMS GET SO STRONG?
HOW DID YOUR GRIP GET SO TIGHT?
HOW, SINCE WE'VE ONLY JUST MET,
CAN THIS FEEL SO RIGHT?

I'M A GIRL WHO LIKES THINGS SIMPLE,
KEEPS THINGS HOMEY
AND IT'S BEST THAT I ADMIT THAT
FROM THE START.
SINCE I HAVEN'T MET A GUY WHO'LL
GET TO KNOW ME
OR CAN SEE THAT I'M OLD FASHIONED
IN MY HEART.

AFTER YEARS OF "IT'S NOT FAIR,"
NOW YOU'VE COME FROM GOD-KNOWS-WHERE!
YOU'RE DIFFERENT FROM THE OTHER GUYS
UNLESS YOU'RE SIMPLY FULL OF LIES,

YOU'RE DIFFERENT FROM THE OTHER GUYS,
AND FOR ME THAT'S RARE!

(The flashback begins to fade as the lights start to change.

MEREDITH *continues singing.)*

The Cemetery, Immediately Following.

(The lights gradually return to the present, as **MEREDITH** *finishes her memory.)*

MEREDITH.
YOU'RE DIFFERENT FROM THE OTHER GUYS
THERE'S SOMETHING SPECIAL
IN YOUR EYES
YOU'RE DIFFERENT FROM THE OTHER GUYS
AND FOR ME THAT'S RARE!

(Music ends. The lights have restored.)

*[***MAN (EDMOND)***" will now be indicated simply as* **EDMOND.** *"]*

EDMOND. You couldn't have forgotten my eyes. Look close.

MEREDITH. I'm trying to.

EDMOND. Can't you see me in them?

(She looks deep into his eyes and almost seems swayed.)

MEREDITH. But nothing else is the same.

EDMOND. You looked so beautiful that night at the bar. You were wearing pink.

(This causes her to "snap out of it" and pull away.)

MEREDITH. A lot of people saw me that night. And I always wear pink. That doesn't prove anything.

(A clap of thunder causes her to reach for the umbrella. She pauses for a moment and thinks. Then she very deliberately makes sure the umbrella passes right in front of **EDMOND**'s *face, as if to test him.)*

EDMOND. You brought my vintage umbrella.

> (**MEREDITH** *doesn't say a word.*
>
> **EDMOND** *notices her hand.*)

EDMOND. You're still wearing your engagement ring.

> *(She doesn't respond.)*
>
> I gave it to you the day of the fire.
>
> *(Her expression seems to say "and?")*
>
> I asked you to never take it off.
>
> *(He tries to reach for her hand. She pulls it abruptly from him and drops the umbrella.)*

MEREDITH. Tell me who you are.

EDMOND. You know.

MEREDITH. I wanna hear you say it.

EDMOND. I'm Edmond.

> (**MEREDITH** *points to the grave.*)

MEREDITH. *(exasperated) That's* Edmond. Edmond is dead. He burned to death. You don't look like him, you don't sound like him. And you don't even have any burns.

> (**EDMOND** *rolls up a sleeve to show his arm is severely burned and scarred.*
>
> **MEREDITH** *reaches, instinctively, to touch it, but stops herself. She just stares at the horrifying sight and remains silent.*
>
> *Satisfied, he rolls his sleeve back down.)*

MEREDITH. That doesn't look so good.

EDMOND. I know. Still hurts.

MEREDITH. *(suspicious)* And yet, your face …

EDMOND. I have a *new* face.

MEREDITH. That is ridiculous.

EDMOND. It's true.

MEREDITH. You look perfect. It would have to be something out of a science fiction movie.

EDMOND. Well, it sort of was like that.

MEREDITH. Fiction.

(Music begins.)

EDMOND. No.

MEREDITH. Face or no face, I was there when Edmond died.

(Unsettled by the memory, she vehemently sings.)

[MUSIC NO. 6 – "IDENTIFIED THE BODY"]

MEREDITH.

I IDENTIFIED THE BODY
THAT'S WHAT THEY CALLED IT.
I IDENTIFIED THE BODY
IN THE MIDDLE OF THE NIGHT.

IT WAS THE HARDEST THING
I EVER HAD TO DO.
AND, BELIEVE ME,
HOW I WISH IT WASN'T TRUE.
BUT I IDENTIFIED THE BODY
AND IT WASN'T YOU.

BOTH.

IT'S BEEN AN AWFUL YEAR
BUT I'M TRYING TO MOVE ON.

MEREDITH.

I'VE ACCEPTED
THAT THE MAN I LOVED
IS GONE.

EDMOND.

HE'S RIGHT HERE...

MEREDITH.

THIS HAS TO BE
SOME KIND OF CON.

(Music continues.)

EDMOND. Meredith, you aren't remembering it right. You "identified me" *before* I died…that is, I *didn't* die. You came to the hospital and they let you say goodbye to me while I seemed unconscious. But they told you I died *after* you saw me. Isn't that right?

(**MEREDITH** *thinks hard and twists at her ring.*

EDMOND *sings.*)

THERE WERE BURNS ACROSS MY BODY
THAT'S WHAT THEY TOLD ME.
AND NOT ONLY ON MY BODY
BUT I BARELY HAD A FACE
AND I BARELY HAD A VOICE.

AND AFTER THEY MADE YOU
LEAVE MY SIDE,
I ASKED THEM
TO TELL YOU THAT I DIED.
THEY LIED.
THEY LIED.

MEREDITH.
THAT ISN'T HOW IT HAPPENED–
THAT'S NOT WHAT I REMEMBER.

EDMOND.
IT'S EXACTLY HOW IT HAPPENED
BUT YOUR MIND IS PLAYING TRICKS.

I WAS IN A LOT OF TROUBLE, AFTER ALL
BUT I WAS FRAMED
AND ABOUT TO TAKE THE FALL.
SO I PAID THE DOCTOR OFF.

MEREDITH.
YOU PAID THE DOCTOR OFF?

EDMOND.
IT WAS MY ONLY CHANCE,
MY BACK WAS TO THE WALL.

BOTH.
IT'S BEEN AN AWFUL YEAR
BUT I'M TRYING TO MOVE ON.

MEREDITH.

I'VE ACCEPTED
THAT THE MAN I LOVED
IS GONE.

EDMOND.

HE'S RIGHT HERE.

MEREDITH.

OR IS THIS SOME KIND OF CON?

(Music continues.)

MEREDITH. You faked your own death? I mean you're saying Edmond faked his own death?

EDMOND. If I didn't, after I recovered I would have been locked up. Even you believed I was guilty. Didn't you?

MEREDITH. The evidence against Edmond was... overwhelming.

(She sings.)

HE DID SOMETHING HORRIBLE.
SOMETHING ON A WHIM.
HE DID SOMETHING TERRIBLE...

EDMOND.

SOMETHING UNLIKE HIM?

(Music continues.)

MEREDITH. Even if you paid the doctor, what about the rest of the hospital?

EDMOND. He took care of everything. Faked some papers, created new records and a new identity for me.

MEREDITH. *(incredulous)* And your face?

EDMOND. *(sings)*

THEN I HAD EXTENSIVE SKIN GRAFTS
GOD, HOW THEY WERE PAINFUL!
EXPERIMENTAL SKIN GRAFTS
I WAS A GUINEA PIG EACH TIME!

AND THEY TOOK A YEAR TO HEAL,
A YEAR OF PAIN.

IT TOOK A YEAR TO FIGURE OUT
HOW TO EXPLAIN.

MEREDITH. Edmond wouldn't have put me through this for a year.

EDMOND. I didn't want you to see me. I needed constant care. I wanted to spare you.

MEREDITH.
BUT I BURIED
EDMOND'S BODY.
WE'RE STANDING RIGHT ABOVE HIM!

EDMOND.
WHEN YOU BURIED
"EDMOND'S" BODY
THERE WAS NO ONE IN THE GRAVE.

(She looks to the gravestone in disbelief.)

MEREDITH. I watched them lower him into the ground.

EDMOND.
IT'S AN EMPTY COFFIN
THAT'S WHAT I ARRANGED.
IT WAS PAINFUL
BUT WE HAD TO STAY ESTRANGED
AND I KNOW WE CAN'T PRETEND
THAT NOTHING'S CHANGED.

(Music continues.)

MEREDITH. Doctors…hospitals…morticians…gravediggers. My, you've got quite a payroll.

EDMOND. I had no choice.

MEREDITH. And I suppose you paid for everything with all that money.

EDMOND. I never had that money. I had to beg. I had to agree to be a science project. And make a lot of unpleasant promises.

BOTH.
IT'S BEEN AN AWFUL YEAR
BUT I'M TRYING TO MOVE ON

MEREDITH.
I'VE ACCEPTED

THAT THE MAN I LOVED

IS *GONE.*

EDMOND.

HE'S RIGHT HERE.

MEREDITH.

OR IS THIS SOME KIND OF CON?

EDMOND.

IT'S NOT A CON!

I'M RIGHT HERE.

MEREDITH.

BUT I IDENTIFIED THE BODY.

EDMOND.

I'M RIGHT HERE.

MEREDITH.

AND I BURIED EDMOND'S BODY...

(He tries to comfort her, but she pushes him away.)

EDMOND.

I'M RIGHT HERE.

TO FINALLY END

THIS AWFUL YEAR.

MEREDITH.

THIS AWFUL YEAR.

BOTH.

THIS AWFUL YEAR!—

(The music crescendos.)

EDMOND.

THERE'S NO ONE IN THE GRAVE!

(Music ends.

MEREDITH *just stares at him for a moment.)*

MEREDITH. If you're Edmond, where the hell have you been for all this time?

EDMOND. Hiding. Healing. Trust me, you wouldn't have wanted to see what I looked like.

(He moves toward her. She recoils slightly.)

MEREDITH. *(scoffs)* "Trust you"?

EDMOND. And I was piecing everything together to figure out what actually happened.

MEREDITH. And did you?

EDMOND. I did.

MEREDITH. And?

EDMOND. First, say you believe me.

MEREDITH. Not so fast.

> (**MEREDITH** *puts her arms around him, and feels him, trying to ascertain if the size is right as she hugs him.*)

EDMOND. Doesn't it feel right?

MEREDITH. I'm not sure yet.

> (**EDMOND** *sighs, frustrated.*)

MEREDITH. Tell me about your family. Have you seen any of them?

EDMOND. I don't have any family. I was an only child. So was my mother. So was my father. No one left.

> (**EDMOND** *smiles at her, confident that he has passed her test.* **MEREDITH** *still seems unsatisfied and tries a different path.*)

MEREDITH. Does Eric know about you?

> (*He bristles at the mention of that name.*)

EDMOND. Eric is a two-faced son-of-a-bitch.

> (**MEREDITH** *lights up as if she's caught him in a lie.*)

MEREDITH. He's your best friend.

EDMOND. I thought so.

MEREDITH. He was devastated when you…when *Edmond* died. And after what Edmond did. In the office right next to him. Eric was so disappointed in you…in *him*.

EDMOND. I didn't do anything. And you have to trust me. Eric isn't who you think he is.

MEREDITH. Oh, please. I don't even know if *you're* who I think you are. And if you really are Edmond, you'd know that Eric was closer to you than I was.

EDMOND. That's what I thought too. But he was always jealous of me. And of us. I think he was interested in you. Did you ever get that feeling?

MEREDITH. Not while Edmond was alive.

EDMOND. It always seemed like he couldn't get past my success. Remember what I told you he said the night before I proposed?

MEREDITH. I don't remember anything like that.

EDMOND. Sure you do. It was at the office, after a few drinks… Eric had watched me pick out your ring earlier in the day…

(Lights change.)

[MUSIC NO.7 – SECOND FLASHBACK INTRO]

Flashback. An Office. A Little Over A Year Earlier.

(Underscored by music, **ERIC** *enters the flashback, and the two men converse as if they are in their office.*

[In keeping with the possible concept of furniture rising up as if from a grave; **ERIC** *himself could also rise up from the ground on a chair.]*

ERIC *seems cold and somewhat distant toward* **EDMOND.** *)*

EDMOND. Tomorrow, my friend, I'm gonna be an engaged man.

ERIC. That's right.

EDMOND. Mere's gonna love the ring. Let me see it.

ERIC. I don't have it.

EDMOND. Don't tell me you lost it. I gave it to you so she wouldn't see it at lunch.

ERIC. You did? Oh, shit…

EDMOND. Relax. I'm just kidding! It's at the jeweler's being engraved.

ERIC. *(perturbed)* That wasn't funny.

EDMOND. *(lauging)* Calm down.

ERIC. I'm calm.

EDMOND. *(changing the subject)* Everything's finally starting to come together for me.

ERIC. *Finally?*

EDMOND. What do you mean?

(Music begins.)

ERIC. Ed, you've *never* had to worry about anything coming together…

(**ERIC** *turns away from him as if he can't bear to look him in the eye.* **EDMOND** *is at a loss for words.* **ERIC** *sings.*)

[MUSIC NO.8 – "JEALOUSY"]

ERIC. *(bitterly)*

YOU GOT THE LOOKS
AND THE GIRLS
AND THE BREAKS
AND A LIFETIME OF FREE DRINKS IN BARS.

WHILE I GET THE CRUMBS
AND THE TRASH
AND THE FAKES
AND TREATMENT LIKE I CAME FROM MARS.

ALL MY LIFE I'VE WISHED
I WAS MORE LIKE YOU
BUT I KNOW OF ALL THE THOUGHTLESS THINGS
THAT JEALOUSY CAN DO.
SINCE I WOULD DIE IF OUR FRIENDSHIP
WAS THROUGH.
I'LL LET NOTHING COME BETWEEN US
AND I HOPE YOU'LL DO THAT TOO.

YOU GOT PROMOTED
AND I WAS SO PROUD
I KNOW *YOU* DESERVED IT, NOT ME.

NOW I'M YOUR ASSISTANT
AND, BOY, AM I WOWED
EVERY DAY YOU'RE ON FIRE, I SEE!

ALL MY LIFE I'VE WISHED
I COULD BE LIKE YOU
BUT I KNOW OF ALL THE CARELESS THINGS
THAT JEALOUSY CAN DO.
SINCE I WOULD DIE IF OUR FRIENDSHIP
WAS THROUGH.
I'LL KEEP ALL YOUR DARKEST SECRETS
AND I HOPE YOU'LL KEEP MINE TOO.

(**EDMOND** *tries to make a comforting move toward* **ERIC**, *but he is rebuffed.*)

AND IT'S IMPORTANT
I TRY TO GET AHEAD
WITHOUT YOUR HELP.
EVEN IF IT MEANS
LIMITED SUCCESS.
I KNOW YOU'VE ALWAYS BEEN
ON MY SIDE,
MY CLOSEST FRIEND.
BUT YOU MUST LET ME
DEAL WITH MY STRESS.

(*Music continues.*)

EDMOND. Where's this coming from?

ERIC. I'm just telling you how I feel.

EDMOND. It's Meredith, isn't it? I found someone and you're still single.

ERIC. It has nothing to do with her.

EDMOND. Eric, she'll never come between us. Trust me.

ERIC. You say that now.

(**EDMOND** *tries to give him a reassuring look.* **ERIC** *sings.*)

ALL MY LIFE I'VE WISHED
I WAS … REALLY YOU!
BUT I KNOW OF ALL THE RECKLESS THINGS
THAT JEALOUSY CAN DO.
SINCE I WOULD DIE IF OUR FRIENDSHIP
WAS THROUGH.
I MAY NOT BE YOUR PRIORITY
BUT I'M STILL IMPORTANT TOO!

AFTER ALL THESE YEARS OF LOYALTY
I KNOW YOU THINK SO TOO!

(**EDMOND** *tries to go to* **ERIC** *to give him a pat on the shoulder, but as he does this, the flashback ends and* **ERIC** *fades from view [or sinks back into the dirt].*)

The Cemetery, Immediatey Following.

(*The lights restore.* **EDMOND** *returns his focus to* **MEREDITH**, *finishing the story.*)

EDMOND. …And he wouldn't even let me respond.

(*Her skepticism is palpable.*)

MEREDITH. (*sarcastic*) Wow. So, I'm supposed to believe *that's* the real Eric and *you're* the real Edmond. Do I at least get to be the real Meredith?

EDMOND. I know it's hard.

MEREDITH. So what exactly is that you're saying?

EDMOND. Eric framed me.

MEREDITH. (*incredulous*) Because you were more popular than him?

EDMOND. Something like that.

MEREDITH. No way. I don't believe it.

EDMOND. He's responsible for everything.

MEREDITH. That's not possible.

EDMOND. Think of it this way, either the Edmond you loved was a crook and a liar—or it was Eric.

MEREDITH. Are those my only two choices?

EDMOND. I'm not joking. Trust me, I couldn't believe it either. I never imagined he could have done this to me.

MEREDITH. I've spent an entire year with Eric. Getting to know him better. Mourning with him. Crying with him. He's not a criminal.

(From offstage, **ERIC***'s voice is heard calling.)*

ERIC. *(offstage)* Meredith? Mere?

EDMOND. That's Eric. I've gotta get out of here.

(He starts off to hide.)

MEREDITH. Why? He won't know who you are.

EDMOND. Just don't say anything about me. Please. I'm begging you.

MEREDITH. Okay…

EDMOND. Ask him what happened the night I died.

MEREDITH. I'll try.

EDMOND. Then get rid of him.

MEREDITH. No guarantee.

*(***EDMOND*** goes off in one direction as* **ERIC***, without his coat, enters from the other. He comes up behind* **MEREDITH** *and startles her.)*

ERIC. Talking to Edmond?

MEREDITH. *(panicked)* What?

*(***ERIC*** motions to the grave.)*

ERIC. His grave. Remember?

MEREDITH. Oh right. He can still hear me.

(She nervously twists her ring again.)

Wasn't I was supposed to come meet you?

ERIC. I thought you'd be done by now. I was a little worried.

MEREDITH. I'm fine.

(In the distance a flash of lightning and a clap of thunder.)

ERIC. Well, the storm's sure not letting up.

MEREDITH. Wonderful.

(He picks up the umbrella from the ground and hands it to her.)

ERIC. Here.

MEREDITH. Thanks.

(She holds the umbrella and looks up as if waiting for the rain to start.)

ERIC. Have you been thinking of what we talked about?

MEREDITH. A little. But…I wanna talk about the night Edmond died. The night of the fire.

ERIC. Mere, why do you wanna put yourself through that? You know everything.

MEREDITH. I just can't get past it. I wanna think more about what could happen between the two of *us.* But I need to process that night one more time and try to let Edmond go. Please.

(Music begins.)

ERIC. All right. Damn I hate this story.

(He takes a breath and begins.)

It was a few hours after the news about Edmond broke online. I had just seen him a little while earlier and everything seemed normal …

(He sings.)

[MUSIC NO.9 – "NIGHT OF THE FIRE – ERIC'S VERSION"]

ALONE INSIDE THE OFFICE–
STILL SHOCKED AT WHAT HE'D DONE.
GLUED TO THE COMPUTER
I FIGURED HE WOULD RUN.
I TURNED AROUND
AND HE WAS THERE
HE WANTED TO EXPLAIN.

THAT'S WHAT HAPPENED
ON THE NIGHT OF THE FIRE.

AS I'VE TOLD YOU MERE,
IT BRINGS BACK SO MUCH PAIN…

(As the music continues, the lights change.)

Flashback. The Office. One Year Ago.

*(**EDMOND** enters and joins **ERIC** in the office as a flashback is enacted. **MEREDITH** watches intently, outside the flashback area.)*

ERIC. Edmond? What are you doing here?

*(**EDMOND** sings.)*

EDMOND.
YOU HAVE TO LET ME TELL YOU
MY SIDE OF THIS MESS.
I HAD TO STEAL THAT MONEY;
IT'S PAINFUL TO CONFESS.
I KNOW YOU WON'T FORGIVE ME
AND YOU'LL NEVER UNDERSTAND …

*(The lights quickly change to the present, as **ERIC** sings directly to **MEREDITH**, who stands watching as the thunder rages around her in her isolated area.)*

ERIC. *(to **MEREDITH**)*
EDMOND SAID THAT
ON THE NIGHT OF THE FIRE.
AS I'VE TOLD YOU, MERE
HE HAD THE WHOLE THING PLANNED …

*(The lights snap back into the flashback as **ERIC** returns his focus to **EDMOND**.)*

ERIC. *(to **EDMOND**)*
YOU KNOW THAT
I'LL SUPPORT YOU.
NO NEED TO
GIVE ME "SPIN"
I PROMISE YOU
I'M BY YOUR SIDE

> AS LONG AS YOU
> TURN YOURSELF IN.

EDMOND.

> I KNOW I'M IN TROUBLE
> AND IN OVER MY HEAD.
> I GOT A LITTLE GREEDY,
> IT'S BETTER LEFT UNSAID.
> THE ONLY WAY
> THEY'LL PROVE IT
> IS WITH EVIDENCE THEY DON'T HAVE YET.
>
> (**ERIC** *turns to* **MEREDITH** *in the present.*)

ERIC. *(to* **MEREDITH***)*

> EDMOND SAID THAT
> ON THE NIGHT OF THE FIRE
> AS I'VE TOLD YOU, MERE
> I NEVER WILL FORGET!
>
> (**ERIC** *returns his focus to* **EDMOND** *in the flashback. Music continues.*)

ERIC. Let me call the police right now. For your own sake.

EDMOND. *(very threatening)* Don't go near the phone, Eric.

ERIC. *(scared)* Holy shit, Edmond …

EDMOND. There's no need for the police—and, anyway, I think you mean the FBI. But I can totally get off if they don't have anything that ties back to me directly.

ERIC. Edmond …

EDMOND. *(sings)*

> THERE'S NOTHING ON THE SERVERS.
> THERE'S NOTHING ON A DISC.
> I KEPT IT ALL ON PAPER,
> I COULDN'T TAKE THE RISK.
> YOU HAVE TO HELP DESTROY IT
> I HATE TO INVOLVE YOU AT ALL …
>
> (**ERIC** *turns to* **MEREDITH** *in the present.*)

ERIC. *(to* **MEREDITH***)*

> EDMOND SAID THAT
> ON THE NIGHT OF THE FIRE,

HE WAS FILLED WITH FEAR
YET HAD A LOT OF GALL.

(**ERIC** *returns his focus to* **EDMOND** *in the flashback.*
EDMOND *has gotten a large stack of file folders and
starts flipping through the pages.*)

EDMOND. The damned shredder is broken! We have to
burn all of these.

ERIC. Here? Now?

EDMOND. I can't go anywhere. They'll be looking for me.

*(He pulls out a book of matches and continues to
rummage around.)*

How fast do you think these papers will ignite?

ERIC. *(to* **EDMOND***)*

I THINK
YOU'VE GONE CRAZY.
YOU HAVE TO
MAKE THIS END.
PUT THOSE PAPERS DOWN.
AND COME WITH ME
LET ME PROVE
THAT I'M TRULY YOUR FRIEND!

(As **ERIC** *tries to take his arm,* **EDMOND** *violently pulls
away from him.)*

EDMOND.

IF YOU'RE
NOT GONNA HELP ME,
THEN STAY OUT OF MY WAY.
I HAVE TO BURN THESE RECORDS
TO MAKE THIS GO AWAY –

ERIC. Please don't do this …

EDMOND.

YOU'VE HAD YOUR SAY
YOU'VE MADE YOUR CHOICE.
I CAN'T CHANGE YOUR MIND
IT'S YOUR CALL …

*(***ERIC** *turns to* **MEREDITH** *in the present.)*

ERIC. *(to* **MEREDITH***)*
> EDMOND SAID THAT
> ON THE NIGHT OF THE FIRE
> THEN HE LIT THE MATCH
> AND THREW ME OUT.

> *(In the flashback,* **EDMOND** *ignites the papers. He gazes eerily into the flames.)*

> THE FEDS CAME TO THE DOOR –

> *(The flashback begins to end.)*

The Cemetery, Immediately Following.

> *(The lights restore.* **EDMOND** *disappears.)*

ERIC.
> EDMOND LOCKED HIMSELF
> INSIDE WITH THE FIRE.
> AND YOU KNOW THE REST
> DON'T MAKE ME TELL YOU MORE.
> IT'S JUST AS PAINFUL AS BEFORE.

> *(Music ends.*

> **MEREDITH** *wipes away a tear.)*

ERIC. Maybe if I would have helped him, I could have gotten him out. And he'd still be alive. In prison. But alive.

MEREDITH. I've never understood it. It just doesn't sound like Edmond.

ERIC. I didn't understand either, Mere.

MEREDITH. Is it possible that you aren't remembering it correctly? Or keeping something from me?

ERIC. It's the truth. Just like I told the police and the FBI. And the reporters. That night'll be seared into my brain forever.

> *(She twists at her ring. He tries to comfort her.)*

Just let it go, Mere. Nothing can bring him back.

MEREDITH. Of course not.

*(She looks to the gravestone. **ERIC** moves in front of her and blocks it from her view.)*

ERIC. Ready to head home?

MEREDITH. I think I need some more time with Edmond.

ERIC. *(understandingly)* Oh. Okay, then. I'll … go meditate for a while.

MEREDITH. Thanks.

(Distant thunder is heard as he starts off. He looks up at the sky.)

ERIC. Looks like the rain may be starting up again. I left my coat in the car. Can I take the umbrella?

*(He reaches for it. Louder thunder. **MEREDITH** grabs it herself.)*

MEREDITH. You'll have to fight me for it.

ERIC. *(joking)* Okay. So my suit'll be ruined.

MEREDITH. It'll be fine.

(She forces a smile. He kisses her on the cheek.)

ERIC. You know how I feel, Mere. I'd never say something that wasn't true or do anything that would hurt you.

MEREDITH. I know, Eric.

(He moves to leave.)

ERIC. *(exiting)* I'm coming back to get you soon before you catch your death out here.

MEREDITH. That can't happen. It's a myth.

ERIC. *(almost offstage)* At least put *your* coat back on.

*(He's gone. **MEREDITH** stands for a while, thinking and twisting her ring. When she is sure **ERIC** is far enough away, she calls out.)*

MEREDITH. Edmond?

*(**EDMOND** re-enters from his hiding place.)*

EDMOND. It feels good to hear you call me that.

MEREDITH. Right now I don't know what else to call you.

EDMOND. Everything Eric told you was a lie. Everything.

MEREDITH. Of course. You have your *own* story.

EDMOND. Not a story. The truth.

MEREDITH. Okay. Let's hear it.

(*A huge clap of thunder and flash of lightning.*)

MEREDITH. *(shaken)* Damn it.

(**EDMOND** *instinctively goes to comfort her.*)

EDMOND. Don't be scared.

(*He opens the umbrella and stands under it with her. They stay huddled together for a moment. Finally* **MEREDITH** *speaks, half-giggling.*)

MEREDITH. It's not raining.

(*She takes the umbrella and puts it down.* **EDMOND** *comments on her lighter demeanor.*)

EDMOND. See, *that's* the Meredith I know.

(**MEREDITH** *laughs a bit. There is a much louder clap of thunder and she practically jumps into* **EDMOND** *'s arms. She looks deeply into his eyes, almost as if she is about to kiss him. But she doesn't. Finally, she speaks.*)

MEREDITH. *(almost dream-like)* Those eyes.

(*She stops herself.*)

So, tell me about the night of the fire.

(*Music begins. As the thunder continues to roll,* **EDMOND** *gathers his thoughts, and finally sings.*)

[MUSIC NO.10 – "NIGHT OF THE FIRE – EDMOND'S VERSION"]

EDMOND.
FORGET WHAT ERIC TOLD YOU–
EVERY WORD HE SAID!
HE MADE UP
THAT WHOLE STORY.
WHY NOT?
HE THINKS I'M DEAD.

BUT HE'S THE ONE
WHO "KILLED" ME.
AND FRAMED ME,
AND RUINED MY NAME.

THAT'S WHAT HAPPENED
ON THE NIGHT OF THE FIRE.
PLEASE BELIEVE ME, MERE
IT'S ERIC WHO'S TO BLAME.

(The lights change, punctuated by more thunder.)

Flashback. A Year Earlier. The Office.

*(**EDMOND** steps away from **MEREDITH** and joins **ERIC** who has entered to take part in the flashback. **EDMOND** still refers back to **MEREDITH** in the present.)*

EDMOND. *(to **MEREDITH**)*

THAT NIGHT INSIDE THE OFFICE
I CAME TO HIM SO SCARED.
I THOUGHT THAT HE'D PROTECT ME
BUT I WAS NOT PREPARED
TO FIND HIM THERE
JUST SMILING
AT THE PANICKED LOOK ON MY FACE.

THAT'S WHAT HAPPENED
ON THE NIGHT OF THE FIRE.
HE HAD LURED ME THERE
AND TRAPPED ME IN THAT PLACE!

*(Music continues as **EDMOND** turns his attention to **ERIC** in the flashback.)*

EDMOND. *(panicked)* Eric, I know you've seen the news by now. But it's not true. I didn't do anything. I can't figure out what's going on.

ERIC. Can't you?

EDMOND. *(confused)* No. But, I'm innocent. You have to believe me.

ERIC. Of course I do.

 (He sings.)

I HATE TO
HAVE TO TELL YOU
BUT, BOY,
HAVE YOU BEEN PLAYED!
I TOOK YOUR PASSWORD
AND YOUR ACCOUNTS
AND THE MONEY
THAT YOUR CLIENTS MADE.

 *(**EDMOND***'s face turns white as a ghost.)*

I DIDN'T WANT TO HURT YOU
I KEPT THE WHOLE THING CLOSED.
I THOUGHT IT WAS ENCRYPTED,
IT SOMEHOW GOT EXPOSED.
AND NOW I HAVE TO SAVE MYSELF
SO I'VE GOT TO PIN IT ON YOU!

 *(**EDMOND** refers to **MEREDITH** in the present.)*

EDMOND. *(to **MEREDITH**)*
ERIC SAID THAT
ON THE NIGHT OF THE FIRE.
PLEASE BELIEVE ME, MERE
IT'S ABSOLUTELY TRUE.

 *(He returns his attention back to **ERIC** in the flashback.*

 Music continues.)

EDMOND. Eric, you stole the life savings from hundreds of my clients. Most of them are left with nothing. With no way to get it back. It's all gone.

ERIC. It's not gone at all, Edmond. It just belongs to me now.

EDMOND. You'll never be able to spend it.

ERIC. I'll find a way. After all, they aren't gonna be looking into *my* accounts, since you're the one who did it.

EDMOND.

> BUT NO ONE WILL BELIEVE YOU.
> ONCE I SAY WHAT I KNOW
> THEY'LL HAVE TO CHECK MY STORY
> AND THEN THEY'LL LET ME GO.
> I'LL PASS
> A LIE DETECTOR TEST
> WHEN I TELL THEM
> WHAT YOU DID AND HOW!

> (**EDMOND** *refers back to* **MEREDITH** *in the present.*)

EDMOND. *(to* **MEREDITH***)*

> THAT'S WHAT HAPPENED
> ON THE NIGHT OF THE FIRE
> BUT I DIDN'T KNOW HIS PLAN
> LIKE I KNOW NOW.

> *(He returns his attention to* **ERIC** *in the flashback.)*

ERIC.

> ED, YOU JUST DON'T GET IT.
> YOU'LL NEVER
> SAY A WORD
> 'CAUSE YOU'RE NOT
> LEAVING HERE—
> NOT ALIVE.
> LET ME TELL YOU
> WHAT JUST HAS
> OCCURRED.

> *(As* **ERIC** *continues, he gets a thick file folder and waves it in front of* **EDMOND**.*)*

> YOU CAME BACK TO THE OFFICE
> TO BURN YOUR SECRET FILE.
> IT ACCIDENTALLY KILLED YOU—
> SO, NO ARREST OR TRIAL.

> JUST OVERWHELMING
> EVIDENCE
> THAT YOU WERE
> BEHIND THE WHOLE THING!

(*EDMOND* turns to *MEREDITH* in the present.)

EDMOND. (to *MEREDITH*)
ERIC SAID THAT
ON THE NIGHT OF THE FIRE
ONLY HOURS AFTER
I GAVE YOU YOUR RING.

(*He returns his focus to the flashback.*)

EDMOND. You'll never get away with it.

(*ERIC* strikes a match and holds it menacingly over the papers.)

ERIC. Edmond, I already have. You're dead.

(*He moves the match toward the papers and ignites them [flash paper]. In that brief burst of flame, the flashback quickly ends [perhaps with *ERIC* lowering down into the ground]. The lights restore.*)

The Cemetery, Immediately Following.

(*The music continues as *EDMOND* finishes the song to *MEREDITH*.*)

EDMOND.
THEN HE LIT THE MATCH
AND PUSHED ME DOWN.
HE RAN OUT AND LOCKED THE DOOR –

LEAVING ME
INSIDE WITH THE FIRE
AND YOU KNOW THE REST
DON'T MAKE ME TELL YOU MORE.
IT'S JUST AS PAINFUL AS BEFORE.

(*Music stops.*

MEREDITH just soaks it all in for a moment, and finally speaks.)

MEREDITH. How could Eric mastermind something like that? How could he fool you?

EDMOND. He was smarter than I thought.

MEREDITH. How could you have been totally unaware of what he was doing on your system?

EDMOND. He figured out a way to cover his tracks.

MEREDITH. But you're so meticulous. That's why you were promoted.

EDMOND. Somehow he managed. And obviously, I felt like an idiot.

MEREDITH. Those poor people never got a dime back.

EDMOND. I know, Mere.

MEREDITH. *(at a loss for words)* It's just… very hard to imagine Eric doing that to anyone.

EDMOND. But it's easy to imagine that *I* could?

(She doesn't respond.)

Before the night of the fire I never would've –

MEREDITH. *(interrupting)* Look, I'm having my own unusual night. So I still don't know what to think. Or what to believe…or who to believe.

EDMOND. *(firmly)* You have to make a choice.

(She nods.)

What does your gut say?

(She thinks for a moment.)

MEREDITH. But Eric is just as broke as ever. He borrowed eight dollars for the toll this afternoon!

EDMOND. He's hiding the money.

MEREDITH. It doesn't make sense…

EDMOND. It didn't make sense to me either. But it happened. He did it.

MEREDITH. I just can't…

*(**EDMOND**'s cellphone loudly and piercingly rings.*

It causes them to both jump.)

MEREDITH. Good Lord!

EDMOND. It's just my phone.

(He looks at the caller ID.)

EDMOND. This is my doctor, Mere. I have to take it. It's important.

(He starts moving away.)

MEREDITH. What? Where are you going?

EDMOND. Just outside the gate. I won't be long.

MEREDITH. But…

EDMOND. I have to.

*(**MEREDITH** moves to stop him.)*

MEREDITH. Wait …

EDMOND. I'll be right back.

(He answers phone as he exits.)

Yes, Doctor, this is Edmond …

*(Once he's gone, **MEREDITH** turns to Edmond's grave.*

There is another loud clap of thunder and lightning.

MEREDITH *looks up at the sky.)*

MEREDITH. *(scared)* Oh great.

(She twists at her ring.)

I think I've had enough time alone in the cemetery, Edmond. Wherever you actually are.

(Softer claps of thunder are heard off in the distance as music begins.

MEREDITH *grabs the closed umbrella and while clutching it tightly, she turns to Edmond's gravestone and sings directly to it.)*

[MUSIC NO.11 – "THE RIGHT CHOICE"]

MEREDITH.

I NEVER THOUGHT
I'D HAVE SUCH A HARD DECISION

TO MAKE.
A DECISION THAT COULD
CHANGE HOW MY LIFE WILL EVOLVE.

IT'S RARE THAT I FIND
ANY KIND OF RISKS
I'M WILLING
TO TAKE.
THERE ARE PROBLEMS THEY CREATE
AND SOME THEY SOLVE.

THE RIGHT CHOICE
IS STARING ME IN THE FACE.
THE RIGHT CHOICE
IF I STAY ON TRACK.

THE RIGHT CHOICE
IS CHALLENGING IN THIS CASE.
IF I MAKE THE WRONG CHOICE
THERE'S NO TURNING BACK.

(The rolling thunder intensifies.)

WHAT I WANT
IS SEEMINGLY NEAR.
IT'S WITHIN MY REACH –
IF I LET GO OF THE FEAR.

(She moves closer to Edmond's gravestone.)

BUT AM I PREPARED
TO SEE IT ALL THROUGH?
IS IT RIGHT FOR ME?
EDMOND, IS IT RIGHT FOR YOU?

THE RIGHT CHOICE
IS LOOKING ME IN THE EYE.
THE RIGHT CHOICE
IF I STAY ON TRACK.

THE RIGHT CHOICE–
IT'S THE MOMENT TO DO OR DIE.
IF I MAKE THE WRONG CHOICE,
THERE'S NO TURNING BACK.

I WON'T MAKE
THE WRONG CHOICE–

(She walks away from grave.)

BUT THE RIGHT LINE OF ATTACK.

(Music ends. The thunder subsides.

MEREDITH, *puts down the umbrella and pulls herself together as* **EDMOND** *re-enters.)*

EDMOND. Sorry, Mere. The doctor had some final test results.

MEREDITH. Test results?

EDMOND. Just some tissue scans. It's been a long process, but I'm gonna be fine.

MEREDITH. That's good.

(She takes a breath.)

I have to tell you something.

EDMOND. What?

MEREDITH. *(overcome with emotion)* I believe you.

EDMOND. *(thrilled)* You do?

(She breaks down and cries.)

MEREDITH. Edmond … I dreamed you weren't dead.

EDMOND. *(comforting her)* Shh. It's okay.

MEREDITH. *(wiping away tears)* After everything …

(She hugs him.)

It really is you.

EDMOND. Of course it is.

MEREDITH. I always felt something wasn't right. I knew you couldn't have been a thief.

EDMOND. I'm sorry you had to be alone this year.

MEREDITH. We have go to the police and tell them everything.

EDMOND. We can't. It's too dangerous for me.

MEREDITH. But you're completely innocent.

EDMOND. You don't understand. There's nothing. No proof. He cleared his footprints perfectly when he burned everything. Nothing on the old system. Nothing in his apartment.

MEREDITH. You were in his apartment?

EDMOND. I was everywhere. And there is *nothing.* No way to clear my name, no way to prove what he did. If the cops or the FBI or the SEC find out I'm alive they're gonna come after me.

MEREDITH. I guess that's true.

EDMOND. I'm gonna have to live the rest of my life in disguise. And he has to pay.

MEREDITH. What do you suggest we do?

EDMOND. We have to get rid of him.

MEREDITH. Get rid of him?

EDMOND. We have to *kill* him.

MEREDITH. *(taken aback)* What?!

(She pulls away from him. He just looks at her seriously.)

MEREDITH. I thought you just wanted to expose him.

EDMOND. That's not enough. He could still turn everything around on me, and I'd end up exactly where I started when this all began.

(More thunder.)

MEREDITH. *(frightened)* We're not killing him.

EDMOND. Meredith, what I haven't told is … *you're* in danger.

MEREDITH. How am *I* in danger?

EDMOND. He thinks you know something.

MEREDITH. Well, I know something *now!*

EDMOND. No, he thinks you have proof.

MEREDITH. Me? What could I possibly have?

EDMOND. He thinks I told you something last year. Or gave you something.

MEREDITH. What?

EDMOND. Over the past few months, I found out that he wasn't sure that I didn't know the truth about him. He thought maybe I had kept some kind of evidence. A USB stick…a portable drive. And he thinks you might have it now.

MEREDITH. You know you didn't give me anything like that. You never said a word.

EDMOND. Of course I didn't. I had no idea what he was up to. But *he's* not sure.

MEREDITH. *(trying to remain calm)* It doesn't matter. I don't have anything.

EDMOND. He thinks you could be playing him. Working with the authorities. Gaining his confidence so you can help catch him. Did he hug you earlier?

MEREDITH. Yes.

EDMOND. He could have been checking to see if you were wearing a wire.

MEREDITH. That's absurd.

EDMOND. No it isn't. He's not gonna let you get very far. He can't have any loose ends. Do you understand what he'll do to you?

(She gasps in astonishment.)

MEREDITH. But he's wrong.

EDMOND. *You* know that. But he doesn't. That's why we have to take care of him first. There's no other way. And once he's dead, I can try every trick I know to find that money and make sure it goes back to everyone it belongs to.

MEREDITH. You really think you could do that?

EDMOND. It won't be easy. But, like you said, I'm meticulous. He was just my assistant.

MEREDITH. We would get caught.

EDMOND. I'm already dead and you have no apparent motive.

*(**MEREDITH** reluctantly nods.)*

EDMOND. Does anyone know you two were coming here tonight?

MEREDITH. No.

EDMOND. Then there's no reason for anyone to question you. Or check here.

MEREDITH. You mean kill him *tonight?*

EDMOND. It has to be tonight.

MEREDITH. Why?

EDMOND. Otherwise he's going to make a move on you.

MEREDITH. How do you know?

EDMOND. Whose idea was it for you two to come here tonight all alone? To a dark, empty cemetery. Yours or his?

MEREDITH. His. We've been planning it for weeks.

EDMOND. He's lured you into a trap. We have to turn the tables on him.

MEREDITH. This is insane. What would we even do with the body? Did I really just say that?

(**EDMOND** *turns and points to the grave.*)

MEREDITH. *(stunned)* No.

EDMOND. Well, it's empty, after all.

MEREDITH. Bury him in *your* grave?

EDMOND. It's where he deserves to be.

MEREDITH. But wouldn't it look obvious if the grave was dug up and re-covered?

EDMOND. Not in the storm. By tomorrow morning everything will be muddy…and we can put some leaves over it. And besides, hardly anyone ever comes here. Almost every other plot is decades old.

MEREDITH. You suggest we dig a grave with our bare hands?

EDMOND. There's a shovel in my car.

MEREDITH. *(stunned)* You're prepared for this.

(**EDMOND** *remains silent.*)

MEREDITH. I can't do it.

EDMOND. It's the only way.

MEREDITH. Someone'll find out.

EDMOND. There won't be any proof that he's even dead. He'll just disappear.

MEREDITH. Forever.

EDMOND. Forever.

MEREDITH. *(almost pleading)* Why can't I just tell him that I don't have what he wants?

(Music begins.)

EDMOND. He won't believe you. And it would blow the whole thing open. Then he'd have all the cards. He had no problem killing me, Meredith. He'll have no problem killing you too. I know it. Trust me.

(He gently sings.)

[MUSIC NO.12 – "NEVER LET HIM HURT YOU"]

EDMOND.

PROTECTING YOUR LIFE
IS MY ONLY CONCERN.
I'VE BEEN WATCHING HIM FOR MONTHS
BUT COULDN'T TELL YOU
WHAT I'D LEARN.
IT WAS SO DIFFICULT,
TRUST ME.

AND RECLAIMING THE PAST
ISN'T ONLY A SCHEME
'CAUSE WE HAVE THE OPPORTUNITY.
I KNOW
IT SOUNDS EXTREME.
IT'LL BE DIFFICULT–
TRUST ME.

'CAUSE I WOULD
NEVER LET HIM HURT YOU.
YOU'RE IN TROUBLE,
'CAUSE HE ISN'T
WHO YOU THINK.
SO WE HAVE TO STOP HIM NOW.

AND THERE'S ONLY ONE WAY HOW.
THEN THIS NIGHTMARE
WILL BE OVER IN A BLINK.

DEFENDING US BOTH
IS OUR ONLY WAY OUT.
HE WILL ALWAYS BE SUSPICIOUS
AND WE'LL ALWAYS
LIVE IN DOUBT
THAT WOULD BE DIFFICULT,
TRUST ME–

YOU ALWAYS USED TO!

I WOULD
NEVER LET HIM HURT YOU.
HE'S BEEN FOOLING YOU
JUST LIKE HE FOOLED ME THEN.
SO WE HAVE TO STOP HIM NOW
AND THERE'S ONLY ONE WAY HOW.
THERE MAY NEVER BE
A CHANCE LIKE THIS AGAIN.

(She tries to turn away but he stops her.)

YOU THINK IT'S DRASTIC
BUT I CAN'T AGREE.
WE HAVE TO HURRY,
HE MAY RECOGNIZE ME.
IF IT'S A CLEAN SLATE
THAT YOU'RE AFTER
IT WON'T COME WITHOUT A PRICE.
YOU'LL BE SAFE,
WE'LL BE TOGETHER,
SO DON'T THINK ABOUT IT TWICE.

AND I WOULD
NEVER LET HIM HURT YOU
BUT YOU MUST KNOW
HE'S A VERY DANGEROUS MAN.
YOU WILL LIVE YOUR LIFE
IN FEAR
IF WE DON'T MAKE HIM

DISAPPEAR.

THERE'S NO OTHER WAY TO DO IT.
BE STRONG, I KNOW YOU CAN!

(He embraces her as the song ends. She takes a moment, and then carefully and confidently responds.)

MEREDITH. Okay.

EDMOND. Okay?

MEREDITH. I'll do it. We have to be together. And never have to worry about him hurting either one of us.

*(***EDMOND*** *appears relieved.)*

EDMOND. It's the only way.

MEREDITH. How do we do it?

EDMOND. He's coming back here soon, I'll hide behind the gravestone and get him from behind.

MEREDITH. Get him how?

EDMOND. I'll strangle him.

MEREDITH. Oh, my God…

EDMOND. There won't be any blood, nothing to clean up.

MEREDITH. Are you strong enough to do it?

EDMOND. Compared to Eric, I certainly am.

*(***MEREDITH*** *takes a moment to contemplate.)*

MEREDITH. What do I do?

EDMOND. Just distract him until I can get my hands around his throat.

MEREDITH. You make it sound so simple.

*(***EDMOND*** *looks her in the eye, and replies in a deadly serious tone.)*

EDMOND. He killed me. He *burned* me. He deserves it.

*(***MEREDITH*** *slowly nods her head.*

From off in the distance, **ERIC** *is heard calling. It startles them both.)*

ERIC'S. *(offstage)* Mere, come on we need to start heading back to the city …

EDMOND. *(whispering)* Shit, here he comes.

MEREDITH. *(whispering)* I'm not ready.

(**EDMOND** *puts a finger to her lips and hides behind the Edmond gravestone. He gives her a "you'll be fine" signal.*

ERIC *enters.*)

ERIC. Hey, looks like we're gonna be chasing the storm all the way home. We should get on the road.

MEREDITH. I… I don't wanna leave yet.

ERIC. Mere, come on. You don't need to stay here. It's starting to give me the willies.

MEREDITH. Why? Are you afraid you might see Edmond's ghost?

ERIC. That's not funny.

MEREDITH. Isn't he haunting you already?

ERIC. What?

MEREDITH. I know what you did, Eric.

ERIC. I don't understand.

(She tries to reason with him.)

MEREDITH. Eric, admit it and maybe we can all come to an agreement.

(**EDMOND** *pops up from behind the gravestone, out of* **ERIC**'s *sight.*

He gives **MEREDITH** *an angry look.*)

ERIC. What are you talking about?

(**EDMOND** *grabs him from behind.*)

EDMOND. You know exactly what she's talking about!

(**ERIC** *struggles in* **EDMOND**'s *grasp.*

MEREDITH *doesn't move.*)

ERIC. Who the fuck are you!?

(He tried to reach to **MEREDITH**.*)*

Meredith!

EDMOND. It's me, Eric. And I told her exactly what you did to me.

ERIC. Who?

EDMOND. Edmond.

ERIC. *(struggling)* That's impossible, Edmond is dead.

EDMOND. Yeah, it was a nice try but you failed.

ERIC. Meredith, what's going on?

MEREDITH. I know the truth now.

(He continues to struggle, but **EDMOND** *holds him tight.)*

ERIC. What truth?

MEREDITH. You stole the money and thought you killed Edmond.

ERIC. I didn't do anything. I told you what happened.

EDMOND. You lied!

ERIC. *(desperate)* I didn't lie. Meredith you have to listen to me. I don't know what's going on. I don't know who this guy is, but I know Edmond is dead!

EDMOND. Stop talking to her!

*(***EDMOND** *turns* **ERIC** *around so they are face to face.)*

ERIC. You're not him.

(He pleads to **MEREDITH**.*)*

He isn't telling the truth. You have to believe me.

*(***MEREDITH***'s confidence begins to waver.)*

MEREDITH. I … don't believe you…

(She looks to **EDMOND**, *as* **ERIC** *keeps trying to break free.)*

Edmond…I don't know anymore… I…

EDMOND. Meredith, he's lying to you and this is *over*!

(**EDMOND** *begins to strangle* **ERIC** *very hard.* **ERIC** *tries to fight back, but it is difficult.*

MEREDITH *now seems unsure.*)

MEREDITH. Wait...stop ... no...

ERIC. *(choking)* Help me, please ...

EDMOND. Meredith, he's lying! He's lying!

ERIC. *(desperate)* I'm not lying!

(**EDMOND** *addresses* **ERIC**, *angrily.*)

EDMOND. Tell her you did it! She deserves the truth once and for all before you're dead.

ERIC. No...

(**ERIC** *struggles and tries to resist and refuse for as long as he can.*)

EDMOND. Tell her!

ERIC. Edmond's dead!

(**EDMOND** *starts getting more and more forceful.*)

EDMOND. Tell her!

ERIC. *(hardly able to speak)* Meredith...please...

(**MEREDITH** *can hardly contain herself.*

EDMOND *tightens his grip.*)

EDMOND. *(screaming)* Tell her!

(He strangles **ERIC** *harder.)*

MEREDITH. No!!! Stop!!!

(She runs to them and tries to pull **EDMOND**'s *hands away.* **ERIC** *reaches for her.)*

EDMOND. Mere, be careful!

(**EDMOND** *squeezes* **ERIC**'s *throat as hard as he can.*)

Tell her the truth, you son-of-a-bitch!

(**ERIC** *finally gives in.*)

ERIC. *(barely audible)* I... I did it.

EDMOND. What's that?

ERIC. *(forcing the words out)* I… I…set the fire…I stole the money…I did it all.

EDMOND. Thank you.

*(Despite the gruesomeness of the situation, **MEREDITH** practically breathes a sigh of relief.*

__MEREDITH__ and __EDMOND__ just look to each other, traumatized, for a moment as __ERIC__ can barely breathe.

__EDMOND__ moves to finally finish __ERIC__ off, but he is distracted by a clap of thunder and lightning.)

[MUSIC NO.13 – FIGHT UNDERSCORE]

(__ERIC__ breaks free.

__MEREDITH__ screams.)

EDMOND. Meredith, run!

(As she does, __ERIC__ rushes for her and blocks her way; __EDMOND__ runs to defend her.

Amidst dramatic thunder and lightning, a knock down, drag-out, struggle ensues between __EDMOND__ and __ERIC__. __MEREDITH__ helps as much as she can.

__EDMOND__ and __ERIC__ each have the advantage at different points.)

ERIC. *(mid-fight)* Nice face, Edmond!

EDMOND. *(mid-fight)* Thanks to you!

(They continue.)

ERIC. *(mid-fight)* Killing you again—It's like the best déjà vu ever!

EDMOND. *(mid-fight)* Sorry to disappoint you!

(They continue. Finally __EDMOND__ regains the upper hand.)

EDMOND. Look me in the eyes, Eric!

(__EDMOND__ strangles __ERIC__.

__ERIC__'s lifeless body falls to the ground.

EDMOND *rushes to aid* **MEREDITH** *who has been pushed down.)*

EDMOND. Are you okay?

MEREDITH. I'm fine. I will be.

(He helps her up.)

EDMOND. It's over.

(He embraces her. She is shell-shocked and almost frozen.)

MEREDITH. I... I... let you murder him ...

EDMOND. It was self-defense. He attacked us.

MEREDITH. Right.

EDMOND. Relax, Mere. It's gonna be okay. Trust me. We can be together now. And Eric'll never get in our way again.

MEREDITH. I know. I'll be okay.

(Her emotions get the better of her. **ERIC** *tries his best to comfort her. After a moment, she controls herself. She looks toward* **ERIC** *'s body and starts to cry again.*

EDMOND *takes her in his arms and turns her away from the sight of it.)*

EDMOND. Don't look at him.

MEREDITH. *(agreeing)* Right.

(He takes her hand and notices her ring.)

EDMOND. Your engagement ring. We can finally get married.

MEREDITH. *(still rather stoic)* I've still got the dress too.

EDMOND. *(trying to be romantic)* In that case, I think I should propose to you again.

MEREDITH. That would be nice.

EDMOND. Then let's start all over.

(He gets down on one knee and makes a grand gesture to pull her ring off.)

EDMOND. May I?

MEREDITH. I thought you'd never ask.

(*He removes it from her finger. Once it is off and in his hand, he holds it up to the light and looks carefully inside.*

MEREDITH *holds out her finger as if expecting him to lovingly slip it back on.*)

EDMOND. (*almost astonished*) There's the engraving.

MEREDITH. I didn't know you had it engraved. What does it say? Something romantic?

(*She reaches for it, but* **EDMOND** *moves it away.*)

EDMOND. Q14-327-BXW-9801006L3.

MEREDITH. (*seemingly very confused*) Huh? What's that number?

EDMOND. It's the passcode to a locked account. An account hidden behind firewall after firewall, encryption after encryption. Unbreakable.

MEREDITH. I'm not following. What does it unlock?

EDMOND. The money.

MEREDITH. What?

EDMOND. The stolen money.

MEREDITH. I don't understand, Edmond.

(*She starts to move away from him.*)

EDMOND. I'm not Edmond.

(**ERIC** *springs up – he was faking his death.*)

ERIC. *And I'm not dead!*

(*Lighting and thunder.* **MEREDITH** *screams and tries to run. But* **EDMOND** *catches her and pushes her to* **ERIC**, *who grabs her from behind and holds her tightly. Music begins as* **ERIC** *slowly tells her the truth.*)

[MUSIC NO.14 – "REPRISE: NIGHT OF THE FIRE"]

ERIC. Sorry Mere, but I found out too late that Edmond had actually been onto me all along. And he was letting me dig my own grave. He fixed it so I couldn't access the account that I made with his credentials. Where I put all the money that I worked so hard to get. He locked it up in cyberspace. And he was just about to push the send button on all the evidence to prove that he was innocent, and I was not.

(He chillingly sings into her ear.)

SO I HOPE YOU COMPREHEND
THAT'S WHAT HAPPENED
ON THE NIGHT OF THE FIRE.
IT WAS HIM OR ME –
I HAD TO KILL MY FRIEND …

All I had was a book of matches from where we'd eaten lunch.

*(**MEREDITH** turns her head away, not wanting the details.)*

But I forgot to get the passcode first. So as the fire was engulfing him, and he thought there was still a chance I could save him, I tried to force it out of him. But he said there was only one copy, hidden someplace I'd never find…And then, he was dead.

*(**EDMOND** holds the ring up in front of her face.)*

It took me months to put two and two together. Then I remembered he'd had it engraved the day before.

*(**MEREDITH** stares pensively at the ring.)*

I went to the jeweler's, but Edmond had made sure they kept no record of what the inscription said. Sorry.

*(**MEREDITH** struggles in **ERIC**'s fairly weak hold. **ERIC** gives up and turns to **EDMOND**.)*

Take her, please.

*(**EDMOND** immediately rushes in and grabs her from him, maintaining a tight grip.)*

MEREDITH. Why did you have to go to all this trouble?

*(She refers to "**EDMOND**.")*

[Though we now know this **MAN** *is not Edmond, he will still be identified by that name for purposes of clarity.]*

Why did you need *him?*

ERIC. Out of an abundance of caution.

(**ERIC** *gets close in front of her.*)

I couldn't be one hundred percent sure that Edmond didn't tell you about the ring, or about what I did, before I...

MEREDITH. Killed him?

ERIC. Right. You might've figured the police wouldn't believe you. And you could have been so scared of me that you pretended everything was fine whenever we were together. Maybe.

(**MEREDITH** *shakes her head in disbelief.*)

So just in case you told someone else, or wrote something in your will that said: "in the event of my untimely death, check my ring finger – then find Eric," I had to find out what you knew.

EDMOND. And you convinced me you didn't know anything at all.

ERIC. Edmond kept you totally in the dark about everything. Stupid, stupid Edmond.

(*She spits in his face.*)

MEREDITH. Screw you.

(**ERIC** *moves to slap her, but stops himself.*)

MEREDITH. Why didn't you just steal it? Hire someone to rob me?

ERIC. There would have been police reports, insurance investigations. Way too risky. And if you *did* know the truth, I would have been the first person you'd suspect.

(**MEREDITH** *turns her face away in disgust.*)

ERIC. I knew there was only one way to get that ring off your finger.

EDMOND. By trusting the man who put it on you in the first place.

ERIC. We had to get you into a scared, vulnerable position.

EDMOND. And it had to happen fast. You wouldn't have believed I was Edmond for very long.

ERIC. But for a short time, I knew you'd *want* to believe.

MEREDITH. *(struggling to get away)* You have the ring. Just let me go.

ERIC. I'm so sorry, Meredith. I'm in this too deep. I had no choice but to kill Edmond to save myself. And now I'm in the same situation.

MEREDITH. You'd kill me for money?

ERIC. For *a lot* of money. *My* money. I should be able to finally enjoy it after all the trouble I went through to get it. All I lost because of it.

MEREDITH. Please …

*(She tries again to pull away from "***EDMOND***'s" grip.)*

ERIC. But you and Edmond will be together. You'll be with him in his grave!

(Thunder and lightning.)

[MUSIC NO.15 – SECOND FIGHT UNDERSCORE]

MEREDITH. No!

*(She breaks free. ***ERIC*** and "***EDMOND***" run for her. They all struggle. But it is quite different from the earlier one—this time it is two men against a woman, giving it a much more menacing quality.*

*****MEREDITH*** puts up a valiant fight – breaking away, running, being caught again and pushed to the ground, only to rise back up.*

The thunder continues throughout. They ad-lib "Get her!" "Watch out!" "Let me go!" etc. as the fight ensues.

*But ultimately, they both overtake her. As "***EDMOND***" holds down her arms, ***ERIC*** strangles her.*

MEREDITH*'s limp body immediately falls to the ground near Edmond's gravestone.*

*"***EDMOND****" and* **ERIC** *stare at her body on the ground, then at each other.*

No one says a word, and neither of them move.

Finally **ERIC** *slowly walks to "***EDMOND****." They stare at each other, tensely.*

*After a moment, "***EDMOND****" reaches for* **ERIC** *and kisses him on the lips.)*

ERIC. I always knew you were the right man for the job.

(Lights instantly change for a flashback.)

Flashback. Several Months Ago.

(Music begins. **ERIC** *and "***EDMOND****" are together in a private place, sharing an intimate moment.)*

[MUSIC NO.16 – "EDMOND'S EYES"]

ERIC.

IT WAS LUCKY WHEN I NOTICED
YOU'VE GOT MY FRIEND EDMOND'S EYES.
IT'S PROB'LY WHY I LOVE YOU—
THE COLOR, SHAPE AND SIZE.
BUT YOU HAVE SOMETHING
HE DID NOT:
AN OPEN, HONEST MIND.
YOU UNDERSTAND ME–HE DID NOT
THAT'S WHY YOU'RE SUCH A FIND.

I LOVED HIM FOR SO LONG
BUT PRETENDED NOT TO KNOW.
AND THOUGH EDMOND'S EYES
WERE SO STUNNING,
EDMOND HAD TO GO!

WHEN I CHANGED MY WAY OF THINKING,

I LOOKED IN MY FRIEND EDMOND'S EYES
AND DECIDED TO BETRAY HIM
THAT BEGAN THE WEB OF LIES.

OH SURE, I'VE HAD
A FEW REGRETS
BUT NONE REGARDING YOU.
SO MANY PROBLEMS,
MANY DEBTS
ALL THE THINGS I HAD TO DO.

I LOVED HIM FOR SO LONG.
BUT IT SEEMED HE'D NEVER LEARN
AND WHEN EDMOND'S EYES
SENT ME RUNNING,
EDMOND HAD TO BURN!

(**ERIC** *moves in a little closer to him.*)

BUT I'M GLAD
YOU'RE A CARING, LOVING PERSON.
AND I'M A LOT LIKE YOU
IN THAT REGARD.
EVENTUALLY
OUR LIVES'LL BE MUCH SIMPLER.
ALL I NEED IS A LITTLE PATIENCE,
THAT'S NOT HARD.

SO FOR NOW, I'LL LOOK TO YOU
WHEN I NEED MY FRIEND EDMOND'S EYES
AND I'LL TEACH YOU ALL ABOUT HIM–
A SIGNIFICANT DISGUISE.

IT WON'T BE
VERY HARD TO FOOL
AN AUDIENCE OF ONE.
JUST KEEP YOUR FOCUS,
KEEP YOUR COOL!
WE BOTH KNOW
IT MUST BE DONE.

(*"**EDMOND**" nods in agreement as **ERIC** starts to move away from him, lost in his own thoughts.*)

ERIC.

I LOVED HIM FOR SO LONG–
AND I OFTEN WONDER WHY.
AND THOUGH EDMOND'S EYES
WEREN'T TOO CUNNING–

EDMOND HAD TO DIE …
EDMOND HAD TO DIE.

(The flashback ends and the lights restore.)

The Cemetary, Immediately Following.

(They take their places back in the present.

They both look away from **MEREDITH**'s *lifeless body.*

The true personality of "**EDMOND**" – *whatever his name really is, emerges. He is very different than how he presented himself earlier.)*

EDMOND. So the money is ours now?

ERIC. Almost!

(He pulls the tablet-style smartphone from his pocket.)

Give me the ring.

(He hands **ERIC** *the ring.)*

ERIC. *(speaking to the Edmond in the grave)* Edmond, your code was indeed unbreakable. But not un-find-able.

EDMOND. *(referring to the ring)* What would you have done if it wasn't on there?

ERIC. Killed myself.

(Using the code on the ring, **ERIC** *types into the smartphone, as if accessing the account.)*

EDMOND. Wow, you get good data service.

*(***ERIC** *smiles, then struggles a bit to read the engraving.)*

ERIC. It's all so tiny. Is this a "B" or an eight?

*("**EDMOND**" looks at it.)*

EDMOND. B.

ERIC. Damn, I typed an eight.

EDMOND. *(reaching for the smartphone)* Here, let me do it.

ERIC. *(pulling it back)* No, it's complicated to get in even *with* the code. I also have my own passwords and little tricks.

*(**ERIC** continues entering the code as **EDMOND** looks on.*

After a few moments, the smartphone beeps.)

ERIC. It's unlocked.

(He breathes an enormous sigh of relief.)

We're in.

(With the weight of the world off his shoulders, he looks at the screen closely and types a little more.)

The money is in the account.

*(He hugs "**EDMOND**".)*

EDMOND. Amazing!

ERIC. After all this time …

EDMOND. …it was worth it.

ERIC. All I have to do now is move it around. Carefully.

EDMOND. I want something very expensive.

ERIC. Don't worry.

*(As **ERIC** continues to work on the smartphone, "**EDMOND**" rolls up his shirtsleeve, revealing the "burns" on his arm.)*

EDMOND. It's nice to be myself again.

(Carefully he peels the fake latex burns off, and drops them onto the ground. [If this is too difficult to achieve, he can wipe the burns off with a handkerchief instead.])

It's a good thing she didn't ask to see the other arm!

*(**ERIC** laughs.)*

EDMOND. Now what?

ERIC. You need to get the shovel out of the car.

(He tosses him the keys.

*"***EDMOND***" starts off, but then pauses and puts his hand on* **ERIC***'s shoulder for a serious moment.)*

EDMOND. This was harder to do than I thought.

ERIC. *(understandingly)* I know, honey. But it's all over now.

(He notices the two candles, still in front of the grave.)

Why don't I light these candles for the both of them, out of remembrance? We could use a zen moment. Will that make you feel better?

EDMOND. I guess so.

ERIC. Okay. Now go get the shovel.

(Music begins)

[MUSIC NO. 17 – "FINALE: HE CAN STILL HEAR YOU"]

EDMOND. I'll be right back.

(He exits.

The sky seems to have grown even darker as **ERIC** *goes to the candles.*

He kneels in front of the gravestone, gets out his matchbook, and lights each candle slowly and carefully.

Almost like a prayer, he sings:)

ERIC.
> YOU KNOW THAT I HOLD
> RESPECT FOR THE DEAD.
> YOU KNOW THAT YOU'RE
> STILL ALIVE, IN MY HEAD …
>
> YOU DON'T EVER HAVE TO
> BLOW OUT THE FLAME.
> BUT DON'T SHUT ME OUT,
> I'M FEELING THE SAME …

(Music continues and underscores the entire final scene.

As **ERIC** *remains kneeling in front of the candles, there is another clap of thunder and lightning flash.*

With **ERIC** *focused on the candles, in the darkness behind him,* **MEREDITH** *rises up – she was faking her death. The light of the candles cause her shadow to loom large.*

She grabs the umbrella. Staying out of his sightline, she goes directly behind him and pokes him in the back with it. He turns around. Their eyes meet. But, before he can say a word, she plunges the metal tip of the umbrella into his heart with great force.

He gasps and falls backward. More thunder.

The umbrella is still stuck in him. He is in disbelief, clinging to life, gasping for air.)

MEREDITH. Don't be shocked, Eric. I can play dead just as well as you can.

(She rubs her neck.)

You're a horrible strangler. But it made it easier. I was ready for anything. Even if you had a gun. Or a knife.

(She makes a "baseball bat" gesture in the air.)

I'd have knocked it out of your hand faster than you could say "Edmond's vintage umbrella." A whole year of practice.

ERIC. *(confused, gasping for breath)* Mere…

MEREDITH. *(mocking him)* "Couldn't be one hundred percent sure…" ?

(He tries to get up but she pushes him back down with her foot.)

Look where being indecisive has gotten you!

(She brushes the debris from the ground off her clothing and straightens herself up.)

You really thought it was possible that Edmond didn't tell me what you were doing the second he found out? Eric, my friend, Edmond *didn't* keep me in the dark about *anything*. Ever.

(**ERIC** *tries to speak but he can't get any words out.*)

And though I've had the passcode the whole time, what I *didn't* have was access to your account.

(*She picks up his smartphone, which is just out of his reach.*

She types a few strokes, as if transferring the funds.

ERIC *lays dying in front of her, trying to pull out the umbrella from his bleeding chest.*)

And now that you've opened it for me, *I* get to decide what to do with the money. *My* money. My *choice*.

(**ERIC** *gasps for breath as* **MEREDITH** *pulls the blood-soaked umbrella out of his fatal wound. He shrieks in pain.*

MEREDITH *fishes her ring out of his pocket and puts it back on her finger.*)

MEREDITH. By the way, the engraving was my idea.

(*"***EDMOND***"can be heard approaching.*)

EDMOND. *(offstage)* Ya know, we really should've brought *two* shovels.

(**MEREDITH** *quickly gets back into her place on the ground to momentarily "play dead."*

*"***EDMOND***"re-enters with the shovel and drops it when he sees* **ERIC***'s bloody body on the ground.*)

EDMOND. *(panicked)* Eric…my God, what happened?

(*He rushes down to* **ERIC***'s side and clutches him.* **ERIC** *tries, but can't talk.*

MEREDITH *comes up behind "***EDMOND***"and points the umbrella into his back.*)

MEREDITH. Don't move.

(He doesn't move.

She goes in front of him, still wielding the umbrella, and stares him down.

Finally he speaks.)

EDMOND. You…knew?

MEREDITH. I've been waiting for this night for a long time. But *you* were a surprise. A nice touch. But ultimately, just an extra step to get what I wanted.

(With her free hand, she waves the smartphone in his face and shows off the ring, back on her finger. He understands.)

So I was happy to play along.

(He just glares at her.)

And now here we are …

*("**EDMOND**" doesn't say a word. He tries in vain to stop* **ERIC**'s *bleeding. But it is clearly too late.* **ERIC** *is dead.)*

MEREDITH. *(coldly)* So, do me a favor, whatever-your-name-is. Bury him for me. In Edmond's grave. You must know how much Eric was in love with him.

EDMOND. *(in shock)* I…I did…

MEREDITH. Then he can spend eternity with him. Edmond will understand.

(She sings.)

I KNOW THAT HE WANTS
MY HAPPINESS TOO,
I KNOW HE SUPPORTS
WHAT I'D LIKE TO DO …

(She kicks the shovel toward him.)

It was so convenient that I didn't even have to bring my own shovel. I was afraid, in his enthusiasm, Eric might have forgotten to put it in the trunk. Phew!

(She strengthens her grip on the umbrella.)

And if you're thinking about the police, just ask yourself: which one of us will they believe? I could tell them the entire truth up to the part where you both tried to kill me.

(She confidently moves toward him.)

Or, we can both keep each other's secrets.

*(She mimics what "**EDMOND**" said earlier.)*

Since there won't be any proof that he's even dead, Eric will just disappear. Forever.

(She indicates the smartphone.)

He'll still be sending e-mails though.

(She gets right in his face menacingly.)

So think *very* hard, "Edmond"!

*(He clutches **ERIC**'s body and sobs. **MEREDITH** sings to him.)*

HIS PRESENCE IS STRONG,
SO YOU CAN LET GO.
YOU MAY FIND THE CONCEPT STRANGE,
BUT I KNOW
HE CAN STILL HEAR YOU.

(A very loud clap of thunder and lightning—the loudest all night. She looks up to the sky.)

Oh, it's finally gonna rain now.

*(She puts her coat back on. Then she opens the bloody umbrella and stands under it. **ERIC**'s blood glistens on the metal tip. **MEREDITH** watches as a few drops spill down onto the ground.)*

That's the one good thing about rain. It washes everything away.

*(She starts off, leaving "**EDMOND**" dumbfounded, still holding **ERIC**.*

She motions to the candles.)

It'll probably douse those flames.

(**MEREDITH** *starts to exit while humming strains of "He Can Still Hear You" as the music softly accompanies her.*

She stops briefly as she passes **EDMOND** *'s grave. She kisses her hand and touches it to the gravestone, then dispassionately walks away.*

A final clap of lightning and thunder, then the sound [and stage effect, if possible] of heavy rain.

*This causes the candles go out, leaving only the slightest shadow of "***EDMOND***" cradling the dead body of* **ERIC**, *with the shovel laying chillingly nearby.*

Blackout.)

[MUSIC NO. 18 – BOWS/EXIT MUSIC]

(The End.)

AUTHOR'S BIOGRAPHY

Stephen Dolginoff is an award winning, New York based, writer/
composer. He received *Drama Desk Award* nominations for Best
Musical and Best Music; an *Outer Critics Circle Award* nomination for
Best Off-Broadway musical; and won an *ASCAP Music Award* for his
musical THRILL ME: THE LEOPOLD & LOEB STORY. Over 100
productions have followed, including a London "Fringe" production
that moved to the West End for a limited run (*WOS Award
Nomination*). THRILL ME has also been seen in cities all across the
USA including Los Angeles (*Garland Award*), Chicago, Boston, Dallas,
Seattle, San Francisco, St. Louis, Orlando, and Philadelphia; in
Canada (Vancouver & Toronto); in South America (Rio de Janeiro,
Brazil); in Australia (Sydney & Melbourne); in several European
countries (Spain, Germany, Greece, Belgium); and most notably,
in Asia, with long-running productions in both Seoul, South Korea
and Tokyo, Japan. Stephen's musicals BEAUTY SLEEP, ONE FOOT
OUT THE DOOR (*Backstage Bistro Award-Outstanding Book, Music &
Lyrics*) and MOST MEN ARE were all produced in New York City
and around the USA. His musical adaptation of JOURNEY TO THE
CENTER OF THE EARTH; his musical comedy, PANIC, the story
behind the infamous "War of the Worlds" broadcast; and his musical
suspense thriller, FLAMES, have been performed in theatres across
the world. Stephen received a BFA in Dramatic Writing from NYU/
Tisch School of the Arts. His work is published by Samuel French
and Dramatists Play Service. As an actor, Stephen played "Nathan
Leopold" in THRILL ME Off-Broadway and on the Cast Album.

www.stephendolginoff.com

www.ingramcontent.com/pod-product-compliance
Lightning Source LLC
Chambersburg PA
CBHW072152130726
47909CB00004BB/1594